A Day for Rememberin'

INSPIRED BY THE TRUE EVENTS OF THE FIRST MEMORIAL DAY

WRITTEN BY
LEAH HENDERSON

ILLUSTRATED BY
FLOYD COOPER

ABRAMS BOOKS FOR YOUNG READERS

NEW YORK

Dark and sad will be the hour to this nation
when it forgets to pay grateful homage to its greatest benefactors ...
the loyal soldiers who imperiled all for country and freedom ...

— Frederick Douglass, 1871, Decoration Day Speech
Arlington National Cemetery, Virginia

In 1861, the United States of America was torn apart by a civil war, with the northern states (the Union) fighting the southern states (the Confederacy). The North wanted to keep the country intact, both North and South, and to ensure that all people were equal by abolishing slavery. The South did not agree, and these states sought to establish themselves as their own country separate from the North: the Confederate States of America. They also sought to keep slavery. The war was fought for four years until 1865, when the Confederacy surrendered to the Union. The United States remained united and slavery was abolished.

Memorial Day, originally called Decoration Day, was established to honor those who gave their lives while fighting in the Civil War. The holiday has since evolved to commemorate all American military personnel who have died in any and all wars. This is a story of what many consider the first Memorial Day celebration.

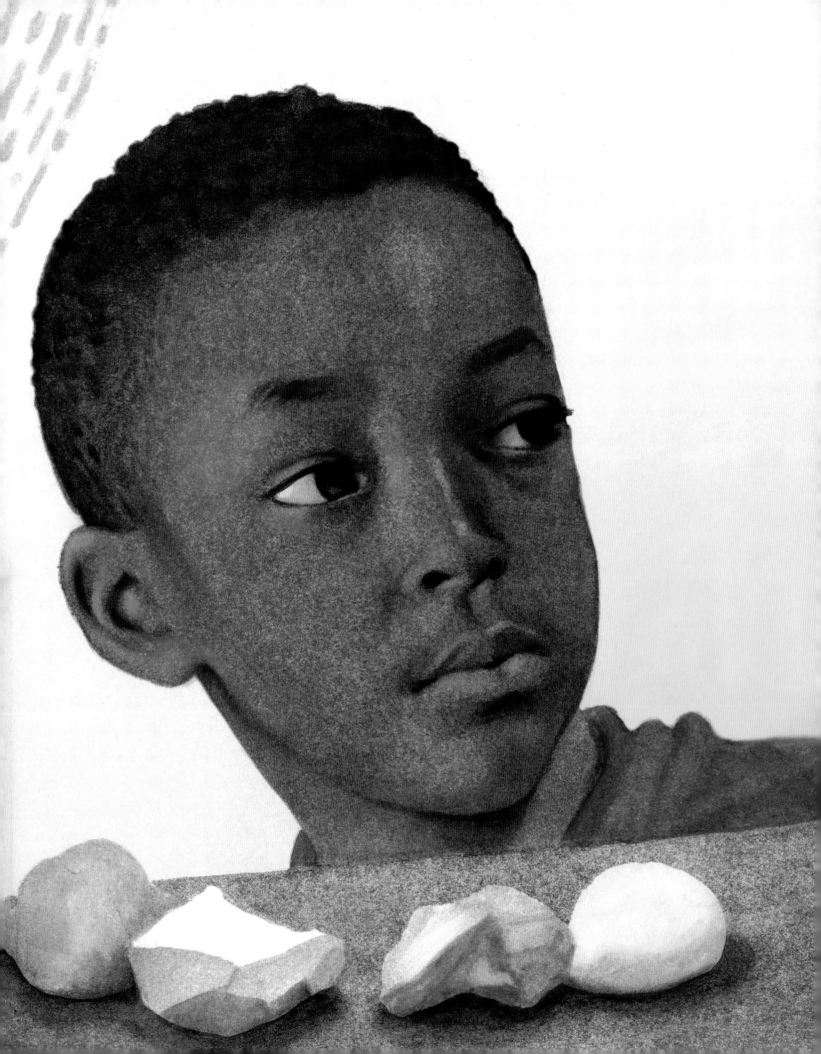

Nine days in a row.

Papa up early and gone again.

I still can't go with him, though. He said, "Eli, school's where you need to be—reading and counting." But I *am* counting. Right here. *Day nine*.

Not following after Papa is harder than holding a hot potato in my hands.

He said important work has to be done—man's work. I rose on my toes then, pushing out my chin, stretching as tall as my ten-year-old self could, but it made no difference.

I imagine him out there standing up to folks who spit in our faces, call us names, or try to run us out our home, mad 'cause we aren't enslaved no more. Or I think of him putting out fires and keeping order with the 21st Colored Infantry. Union soldiers, brown like us, who marched up Meeting Street holding their heads high in victory—especially the ones who'd been enslaved here in Charleston. They were some of the first to come when the mayor surrendered the city to the Union.

No use begging to follow Papa, though. Mama will only fuss, "Eli, you now have the hard-earned right to learn and it's what's gonna get you beyond. Masters locked away learning 'cause knowledge is its own freedom. You're going to school. And no more words are getting spilt about it."

Before the war, worry never let my insides 'lone—
always scared that Mama or Papa would get sold away,
never to come back home. But today, Papa comes home
as night covers the sky. Almost looking worse than
after toiling in Master's fields. But those days in the
fields are over. Papa said unlike some, we aren't going
back because we aren't enslaved no more.

"We were diggin', and buildin', and paintin'," he says
after supper.

"Diggin'? Buildin'? Paintin'?"

But Papa isn't giving no more answers.

"Wake up, Eli. Today you're coming with me."

Day ten! I spring out of bed like beans in a skillet and jump into my breeches. Something important must be happening if Papa is letting me miss even one second of school—my "hard-earned right"—and Mama isn't putting up no fuss.

With molasses-smeared cornbread sliding down my throat, I race to catch Papa. His long strides are met by others as more men join us, their boots crunching against pebbles on the hard road. My new schooling helps me count twenty-eight men in all. Shoulders back, chests out, they stomp along, ready to do the real important business Papa talks about. Business he thinks I'm old enough to do now, too.

"You need to see the work we's doin' before it's all done," he says.

We strut through the entrance at the planter's racecourse, where white folks used to watch mighty horses run before the war. But it isn't a racecourse no more. For a while, the Confederates made it a jail. Mama and ladies from church used to sneak food to the Union soldiers held prisoner there.

Skinny and sickly, those men hardly had more clothes than the most lonesome slave. A newspaper man said those poor souls had "no covering but the sky" and that they were "heartsick, homesick, sick in body, sick in life." All because they fought against slavery and our God-given right to be free.

So over the evening paper, Mama had learned to read in secret while enslaved. She promised, "We'll share every morsel we got till we got no more."

But the living are gone now. And the dead lie by our feet.

Without a word, Papa and the other men get to digging, hammering, and cutting wood.

Papa points to the fence where some of my schoolmates have joined their papas, too. "Help with the whitewashing, Eli."

I drag my feet, though, wanting to stay by Papa's side. But he rushes around doing more work in a minute than he'd done in three hours on Master's land.

An old usher from our church pushes a painting brush in my hand and I get to working, too. As the sun beats our backs, the men sing in heavy, deep voices that rattle the dirt.

Nobody knows the trouble I've seen

Nobody knows my sorrow...

When the sun starts slipping behind the trees, they raise an arch. Tired pinches my shoulders and my palms blaze, crisscrossed with tiny scrapes from a day's hard toil. But I don't pay the sting or ache no mind. We've done good work for the soldiers who lost their lives for our freedom.

The next morning before the rooster's first *gawks*, I leap up—but I'm not going to school again today. None of us colored children are. This day is *that* important.

My best-mended pants and cleanest shirt wait on my blanket.

Mama gathers up her basket full of mayflower bundles, Papa straightens his hat, and we leave our yard just as our neighbors leave theirs. Black faces—more than I've ever seen together—fill the streets with bouquets, crosses, and wreaths.

I'm not sure a flower is left unpicked in Charleston. My schoolmates carry roses and hawthorns. But since I'm fastest at learning my numbers and letters, I get to carry the flag. Right out in front. I stomp, knees high, like the important colored soldiers did up Meeting Street.

Mama strides in her best calico dress behind us with the women. Grinning. Proud. I can't see Papa, but I know he is somewhere in the quilt of black, brown, and white faces.

In lines stretching longer than a mile, we cross onto the old racecourse, singing with our fullest hearts:

John Brown's body lies a-mouldering in the grave but his soul goes marching on.

Although we sing about John Brown, we are really singing for all the buried Union soldiers.

After the last word is sung, quiet comes. Our feet shushing across the sandy soil. We circle the fresh dirt mounds, with sweet-smelling petals of rose, lilac, and jasmine swirling to the ground.

Thousands of hands sprinkle thousands of spring blossoms. The graves become a bed of petals and tears.

The flag flaps in the breeze when I hand it off, as if waving goodbye to the Union soldiers finally at peace.

Pastors preach sacrifice, abolitionists proclaim freedom, and officers bay at us to remember.

Even though we are sad, we are celebrating, too. My heart rests easy now. Me, Mama, and Papa can't never be sold away no more, and I'm getting my schooling—its own freedom, like Mama said. So my insides feel all good.

While breaking bread, we listen to more speeches about the martyrs of the racecourse and freedom. Blurry eyes praise a Union brigade marching 'round the pond of blossoms. There's lots of head-nodding and *mm-hmm*s as families gather 'round the grandstand rememberin', shedding tears, and giving thanks above.

That flag never stops waving. But all my old slave-time worry flies away.

And as the moon joins in, we leave the racecourse with empty hands and near-bursting hearts hoping those Union soldiers, hugged by Charleston's sweetest blooms, know we will never forget what they've given of themselves for the priceless gift of our liberty.

AUTHOR'S NOTE

A few years ago, I stumbled across an image of two hundred or so Black children getting ready for what looked like a parade, and my curiosity was ignited. I did a quick search and found an article about the "first Decoration Day." There are over a dozen places that lay claim to this distinction. However, a story from Charleston, South Carolina, at the end of the Civil War caught my attention—a procession of ten thousand (most newly freed enslaved people) led by almost three thousand Black children. Sadly, it is a moment in our country's history that has not garnered much mention, but for me, a spotlight suddenly blazed bright.

Every year on Memorial Day (originally known as Decoration Day), we remember the men and women in the Armed Forces who died in service to our country, but many may be unaware of its beginnings. Regardless if you believe, as I do, that this Charleston event was the first community-led observance of Decoration Day, it is important to consider the significance of the gesture of these once enslaved people towards the soldiers who'd lost their lives fighting in part for their freedom. Above all else, that May Day was a gathering to honor and to remember those who, as Lincoln said in the Gettysburg Address, "gave the last full measure of devotion."

And we, too, should remember their sacrifice and a community's show of thanks.

These are the children who sparked my curiosity. Although this image is often attached to the May 1, 1865, event in Charleston, South Carolina, it was taken by Frances Benjamin Johnston at the Whittier Primary School in Hampton, Virginia (between 1899–1900).

THE ROOTS OF DECORATION DAY

Charleston, South Carolina, 1865

This is the racecourse club house where Union officers were imprisoned. The enlisted men were kept on the field and were subject to the elements. The photograph was taken in Charleston, South Carolina (April 1865).

In September 1864, during the final years of the Civil War (1861–1865), a well-to-do racecourse in Charleston, South Carolina was turned into a prison for captured Union soldiers. It was said that over ten thousand prisoners had been held in the Washington Race Course at one time, and that the prison was like a "miniature" Camp Sumter in Andersonville, Georgia, one of the worst Confederate prisons. Many of the prisoners were stripped nearly bare on arrival and housed in an open section of the racecourse with no tents or other covering for protection. By the time the prison closed less than seven months later, 257 Union prisoners had died on the grounds due to exposure, disease, and starvation.

In late April 1865, with the North victorious, twenty-eight newly freed men who called themselves the "Friends of the Martyrs" and the "Patriotic Association of Colored Men" volunteered to make a respectful resting place for the fallen Union soldiers who had helped secure their freedom. They reburied the "martyrs" in individual plots and placed a headstone in front of each grave. Over ten exhausting days, the men put the makeshift cemetery in order, erecting a ten-foot-high whitewashed fence with an archway over the entrance gate that read "Martyrs of the Race Course."

On May 1, the first free May Day in the lives of the formerly enslaved, ten thousand people, both Black and white, gathered at the racecourse to pay respect. Nearly three thousand Black children from newly formed freedmen's schools led the way. Countless other newly freed citizens, abolitionists, missionaries, teachers, Union loyalists, officers, and even a few former slaveholders took a place in the procession.

After the children marched and sang "John Brown's Body," "America," "Rally 'Round the Flag," and "The Star-Spangled Banner," every person passed under the archway and scattered flowers over the graves in silence. "When all had left . . . the tops, the sides, and the spaces between them—were one mass of flowers, not a speck of earth could be seen," recalled a special correspondent for the *New-York Daily Tribune.*

A number of ministers, military officers, and abolitionists gave speeches on two separate stages within the racecourse grounds. A full brigade of colored Union infantry marched around the graves and held drills in the inner area of the racecourse. Families spread out across the fields to listen to speeches and picnic into the evening as they honored the fallen and celebrated their newfound freedom. According to a special correspondent for the *New-York Daily Tribune,* this early Decoration Day ceremony was "a procession of friends and mourners as South Carolina and the United States never saw before." *A Day for Rememberin'* is a fictionalized account of these events.

TIMELINE

MARCH 4, 1861   Abraham Lincoln became the sixteenth President of the United States of America.

APRIL 12, 1861   Confederate troops attacked Fort Sumter near Charleston, South Carolina. The American Civil War began.

JANUARY 1, 1863   President Lincoln issued the final Emancipation Proclamation, announcing the freedom of all enslaved people in territories held by Confederates.

SEPTEMBER 1864   The first Union prisoners were brought to the Washington Race Course in Charleston, South Carolina.

JANUARY 31, 1865   The U.S. Congress approved the Thirteenth Amendment to the United States Constitution, which legally abolished slavery.

FEBRUARY 18, 1865   The mayor of Charleston surrendered to Union troops. Many of the white residents evacuated, while many of the former enslaved people and freedmen remained.

FEBRUARY 1865   The war officially ended. The prisoners at the Washington Race Course were freed.

APRIL–MAY 1865   The final surrenders of remaining Confederate troops occurred.

APRIL 14, 1865   President Abraham Lincoln was assassinated.

MAY 1, 1865   Decoration Day. Ten thousand newly freed enslaved people, abolitionists, and others decorated the graves of 257 fallen Union soldiers at the Washington Race Course in Charleston, South Carolina.

JULY 4, 1865   Emma Hunter and Elizabeth Meyer of Boalsburg, Pennsylvania, helped start a remembrance tradition in their small town by decorating the graves of Civil War soldiers, including those who might have had no one to remember them.

DECEMBER 6, 1865   The Thirteenth Amendment to the United States Constitution, passed by Congress on January 31, 1865, was finally ratified by all states. Slavery was fully abolished.

APRIL 25, 1866   While decorating the graves of fallen Confederate soldiers, four women from the Ladies Memorial Association in Columbia, Mississippi, also laid flowers at the unkempt graves of nearby Union soldiers.

MAY 5, 1866   In Waterloo, New York, Henry Carter Wells and General John B. Murray organized a ceremony to honor their community's fallen Civil War soldiers. They called it Decoration Day.

MAY 5, 1868   General John A. Logan, national commander of the Grand Army of the Republic (GAR), called for an annual decoration of graves every May 30.

MAY 30, 1868   Memorial Day was officially observed for the first time at Arlington National Cemetery in Arlington, Virginia, where both Union and Confederate soldiers are buried.

1882   Decoration Day became known as Memorial Day to remember American soldiers lost in all wars, but the name was not officially changed until after World War II.

MAY 17 and 19, 1966   President Lyndon B. Johnson officially declared Waterloo, New York, the "Birthplace of Memorial Day."

JANUARY 1, 1971   The Uniform Monday Holiday Act was passed by Congress, which established that Memorial Day is to be celebrated on the last Monday of May.

APRIL 14, 1971   Memorial Day officially became a national holiday.

OTHER CITIES WITH CLAIMS OF BEING THE BIRTHPLACE OF MEMORIAL DAY

- Columbus, Georgia
- Columbus, Mississippi
- Gettysburg, Pennsylvania

- Savannah, Georgia
- Waterloo, New York
- Petersburg, Virginia

- Carbondale, Illinois
- Boalsburg, Pennsylvania
- Warrenton, Virginia

NOTES

2   "Dark and sad." Speech. "Address of Fredrick Douglass at the Monument of the Unknown Dead, Arlington," Frederick Douglass. *Life and Times of Frederick Douglass: His Early Life as a Slave, His Escape from Bondage, and His Complete History to the Present Time.* Boston, MA: De Wolfe, Fiske & Co, 1895, 505.

15   "No covering but the sky." Newspaper article. "Monument to the Martyrs of the Race Course," *New-York Daily Tribune*, April 8, 1865, 3.

15   "Heartsick, homesick, sick in body, sick in life." Newspaper article. "Monument to the Martyrs of the Race Course," *New-York Daily Tribune*, April 8, 1865, 3.

19   "Nobody knows the trouble I've seen." Words to "Nobody Knows the Trouble I've Seen." First published in 1867 but was a familiar slavery song before the war.

24   "John Brown's body lies a-mouldering." Words to "John Brown's Body," Library of Congress website. See loc.gov/resource/amss.hc00015d.0.

33   "The priceless gift of liberty." Quote by Mary A. Redpath. "Unofficial Memorial Day," *Journal of the Military Service Institution of the United States*, July-August 1910, 118.

35   "Miniature." Diary entry of Esther Hill Hawks, "May Day." Granville P. Conn, *History of the New Hampshire Surgeons in the War of the Rebellion*, Concord, NH: Ira C. Evans, 1906, 290.

35   "When all had left." Newspaper article. "Honor to Our Martyrs," *New-York Daily Tribune*, May 13, 1865, 3.

35   "A procession of friends and mourners." Newspaper article. "Honor to Our Martyrs," *New-York Daily Tribune*, May 13, 1865, 3.

SELECTED BIBLIOGRAPHY

BOOKS

Blight, David W. *Race and Reunion*. Cambridge, MA: Belknap Press of Harvard University Press, 2001.

Clinton, Catherine. *Honoring Fallen Soldiers: America's First Memorial Day*, May 1, 1865. Columbia, SC: South Carolina Humanities Council, 2002.

Conn, Granville P. *History of the New Hampshire Surgeons in the War of the Rebellion*. Concord, NH: Ira C. Evans, 1906.

NEWSPAPERS and JOURNALS

"Honor to Our Martyrs." *New-York Daily Tribune*, May 13, 1865.

"Monument to the Martyrs of the Race Course." *New-York Daily Tribune*, April 8, 1865.

"The Martyrs of the Race Course." *Charleston Daily Courier*, May 2, 1865.

"Decoration Day." *The American Missionary*, Vol. 14, July 1870.

VIDEOS

"Roots: The History of Memorial Day." The History Channel.
See youtube.com/watch?v=3JdutFaLSvw.

"American Experience: Memorial Day." PBS.
See pbs.org/video/abolitionists-memorial-day.

For Grandpa Eddie and in remembrance of all those
who have fought and continue to fight for liberty
—L.H.

For the Little Ones to know, and remember . . .
—F.C.

Author's Note: My choice to drop the "g" at times has everything to do with the rhythm of a people's words.
My people. A rhythm rooted within a rich and heart-filled Black vernacular. In *The People Could Fly*, Virginia
Hamilton writes that her word choices "reflect the expressiveness" of the original Black storyteller, and through
my choices, I hope to do the same. *A Day for Rememberin'* is all about a people's abundant expression.

The illustrations made in this book were made by oil erasure.

Photo credits: Page 34 and 35 courtesy of the Library of Congress.

Cataloging-in-Publication Data has been applied for and may be obtained from the Library of Congress.

ISBN 978-1-4197-3630-8

Text © 2021 Leah Henderson
Illustrations © 2021 Floyd Cooper
Edited by Howard W. Reeves
Book design by Heather Kelly

Printed and bound in China
10 9 8 7 6 5 4 3 2 1

Abrams® is a registered trademark of Harry N. Abrams, Inc.

ABRAMS The Art of Books
195 Broadway, New York, NY 10007
abramsbooks.com